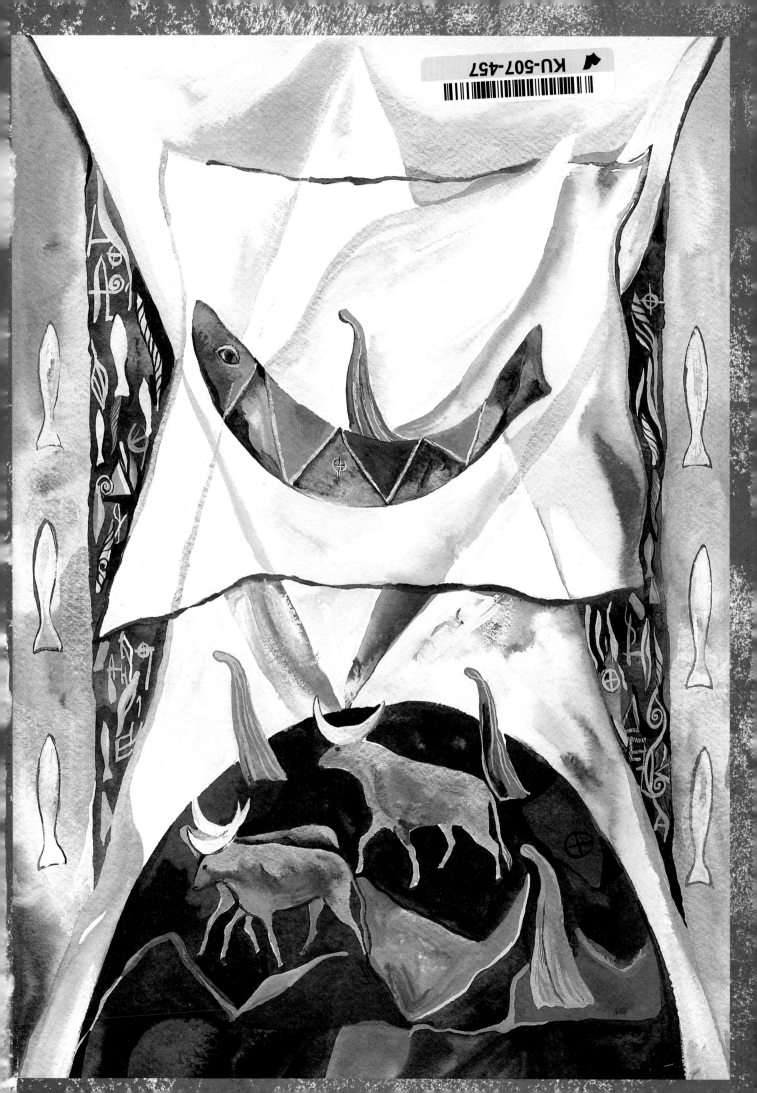

Written by Ewan Allinson
Illustrated by Maria Rud

First published in Great Britain 1998 by DOM
30 St. Mary's Street, Edinburgh

Graphic Design by DOM
Production coordination, computer realisation and colour separation
by Yasnaya Polyana Publishing House, Tula, Russia
Printed and bound by Detskaya Kniga, Moscow, Russia

ISBN: 0 9532710 0 5

To Calum
   and Neil
   - for chasing rainbows.

          Ewan Allinson

From - Grandad & Grandma
          Inverness

          February 2001

(after meeting Ewan Allinson, the author, in
his premises, Dom Art Gallery, 8 Advocates' Close,
off High St. (The Royal Mile) Edinburgh. He is a
Lakeland man (Cumbrian) - I recognised the accent)
Darlington - parents from

THE LOST RAINBOW

ne morning, the Calfcockerel awoke with sadness in his soul. How it had got there was a mystery to him. But there it was.

He stumbled out from beneath the tree where he had been sleeping and shook his tail feathers.

"What to do?" he muttered.
"What to do?" the world murmured in quiet reply.

There was nothing else to do but walk, so he walked until he came to a river. It was a wide river flowing idly towards a distant town and from there out to sea. Even the river was a little sad.

As the Calfcockerel bent down to drink, a fish darted from beneath a rock and then swayed among the reeds in the clear water.

"I suppose the fish is never sad," thought the Calfcockerel as he slurped a little water.

He stood up, took his violin and began playing, hoping his melodies might chase the sadness away. But he played badly and this only made him feel worse. He shook his bowed head and pleaded:

"Dear Violin, you must forgive me for being so very useless. I was a fool to think that I could ever play you with these stupid heavy hooves of mine."

The fish had been listening with great interest to the musician's gloomy words. Being very wise, she could not feel sorry for the Calfcockerel. She did want to help though. She climbed out of the river and walked over to him.

said the fish.

The Calfcockerel glanced doubtfully at this stranger. He grudgingly muttered "hello" and then proceeded to sulk.

The fish continued:

"I'm on my way to a peculiar place. Would you like to come?"

The Calfcockerel did not answer at first. He really wanted to be on his own. But then again, how could he resist an adventure to some unknown place? It was impossible for him to refuse. With a half-smile, he nodded to the fish and off they went.

The musician threw the violin over his shoulder and tried to keep up with the fish who was disappearing up the river.

s they travelled, the river got younger and the mountains closer. By evening they had come to the foot of the mountains. From upon high, almost as high as the clouds, tumbled the biggest waterfall the Calfcockerel had ever seen. As they were tired, they curled up beneath a rowan tree and slept.

At Dawn, the fish awoke and whispered to the Calfcockerel: "Come, we must continue to this river's source, up on this mountain."

The Calfcockerel opened his weary eyes and looked up to the top of the waterfall. He could not imagine how they would ever climb up such a steep slope. But he trusted the fish and followed her.

Squeezing between thick bushes, they climbed onto some slippery steps that led into a cave behind the waterfall.

Carefully, very carefully, the Calfcockerel made his way up the steps into the cave.

Outside of the cave, the noise of the waterfall had filled the air. Inside the cave there was almost complete silence but for the quiet echo of drips dropping. He shivered within and wished more than anything to be back out in the open air, dozing in the morning sun.

He turned to tell the fish that he was going back out but she was already disappearing up some steps at the back of the cave. Not wanting to lose his new friend, he ran after her.

The steps went on and on and on, lit by torches hanging from the walls.

On and on they climbed.
And on and on.
And on.

At long last, the steps brought them back into daylight. The beautiful dawn which they had left behind at the foot of the waterfall was nowhere to be seen.

The sky was covered with low cloud. All was dark and dismal. A cold wind whistled around them and the Calfcockerel shivered as he had when he entered the cave.

"Come this way," said the fish.

The musician followed, squeezing between two carved boulders. They found themselves on the side of a secret valley perched high in the mountains.

In the middle of this valley was a lake as dark as ink. Beyond the lake stood a village where grey figures walked bent against the cruel wind.

Turning his gaze up to the head of the valley, what the Calfcockerel saw truly amazed him.

There, over the source of the river, stood a frozen rainbow. Its broad grey arch straddled the valley, its crest was lost in the clouds.

"Come," said the fish. "It is to the rainbow that I must take you."

As they walked, the fish told the Calfcockerel the story of the rainbow.

THIS VALLEY HAD ONCE BEEN A PARADISE

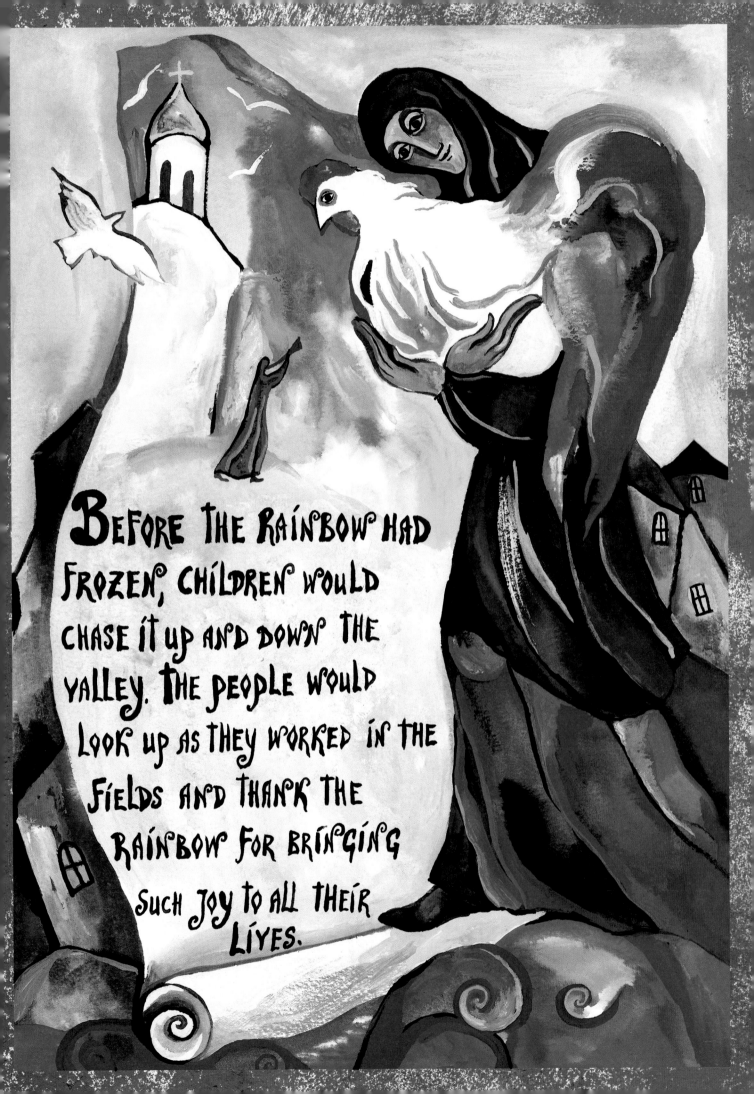

BEFORE THE RAINBOW HAD FROZEN, CHILDREN WOULD CHASE IT UP AND DOWN THE VALLEY. THE PEOPLE WOULD LOOK UP AS THEY WORKED IN THE FIELDS AND THANK THE RAINBOW FOR BRINGING SUCH JOY TO ALL THEIR LIVES.

But there came a time when people stopped noticing the rainbow.

They started caring more about the pieces of silver and gold which they got for selling wool in the Lowland markets. When the children spoke about the rainbow, the people would say, "Huh, what use is the rainbow to us? You cannot put it in your pocket like this silver coin and you cannot sell it at the markets like this wool. What use is the rainbow to us?"

When the older children heard this they felt foolish for ever having loved the rainbow.

Bit by bit, all the children stopped chasing the rainbow and so the rainbow just stayed in one place, at the head of the valley. It stayed there and never moved.

Then one day, a thick bank of cloud rolled over the valley and a cold cold wind started to blow.

"The rainbow froze" explained the fish,

"and everyday since has been just like this one. The poor children just stay indoors all day."

y now they had come to the foot of the rainbow and as the Calfcockerel stood staring, his ears stood up to the sound of a mournful humming. He stooped closer to the rainbow's column of ice. From deep inside the ice came the whispers of a strange music so sad and slow. The Calfcockerel shivered within as the music touched his soul. The fish smiled as the Calfcockerel picked up his violin. At first he just listened. Then he began to play. The notes he played were so quiet that it was impossible to tell them apart from the hum of the rainbow. He closed his eyes to hear better and began playing a melody so gentle and tender that the wind and clouds stopped to listen. Deep within the rainbow's ice a melody stirred, more beautiful than that which the musician had just played. It became louder and clearer.

As the fish watched, a ribbon of deep red rose up the inside of the rainbow to shoulder height, melting the ice in its path.

As the red wavered there, the music from the ice became more joyous. The Calfcockerel answered with a melody more spirited than had ever been heard by human ears. As he played, ribbons of orange, yellow and green climbed up to the same height as the red and wavered there.

The people of the village, surprised by the sudden dying of the wind, looked towards the rainbow and heard the music. Everyone came out of the houses and stared. The children started running around the lake to get closer.

The music had now become less playful, more earnest. The rainbow and the musician were being drawn by the music towards distant shores of storm and serenity. A blue glow appeared beside the rainbow's green and climbed.

The rainbow fell silent. The people of the village gasped and prayed for the Calfcockerel to finish his magic.

The Calfcockerel was absolutely still, listening to the silence of the rainbow, the people and the valley. His hooves found and held the note which echoed the silence perfectly. Holding that one note, he let it ebb and flow, come and go, reaching further and further into its heart until slowly, the indigo and violet rose up the rainbow's outer edge like swirling mists.

When the violet reached the same height as the other colours, a golden ray of sunlight caught the rainbow's crest and the colours flashed across the arch to the rainbow's far end. The clouds broke up and the villagers cried to see the beauty of a blue sky.

All the children ran as fast they could towards the rainbow, but however fast they ran, they never seemed to get closer. Before long, they stopped their chase and rolled down the slopes in fits of laughter.

The fish and the Calfcockerel could hear the laughter as they squeezed between the two carved boulders which led to the secret staircase. When they got to the cave below, the awful silence was gone, shattered by the mighty roar of the waterfall. Outside the cave it was a beautiful breezy afternoon. The Calfcockerel sat by the edge of a pool while the fish idled in the shallows just below.

After a while the Calfcockerel asked:

"Can we maybe travel together for a while, that is if you don't mind?"

The fish stood up and saying neither yes or no, spoke thus:

"Many musicians have passed by this way and for none of them did I ever climb out of this cool clear water. Thanks to you, all is well now with this river. My work is done and I must return to the the ocean. But before I go, may I ask one more thing of you?"

"Of course," answered the Calfcockerel, "of course."

The fish continued:

"Whenever you find yourself beside a river or the sea, play your music and the water shall bring it to me. When I hear those melodies, I will know you are well. One day it will help lead me back to you, for I know we shall meet again."

"I will so look forward to that day," replied the Calfcockerel.

The fish bowed and with a glance of silver was gone.

The Calfcockerel rolled onto his side and closed his eyes. "When I wake I shall play and even though the fish will probably be in the ocean by then, it will be like she is here with me."

With that thought, the Calfcockerel dozed off and as he slept, the last remaining drops of sadness left his soul.

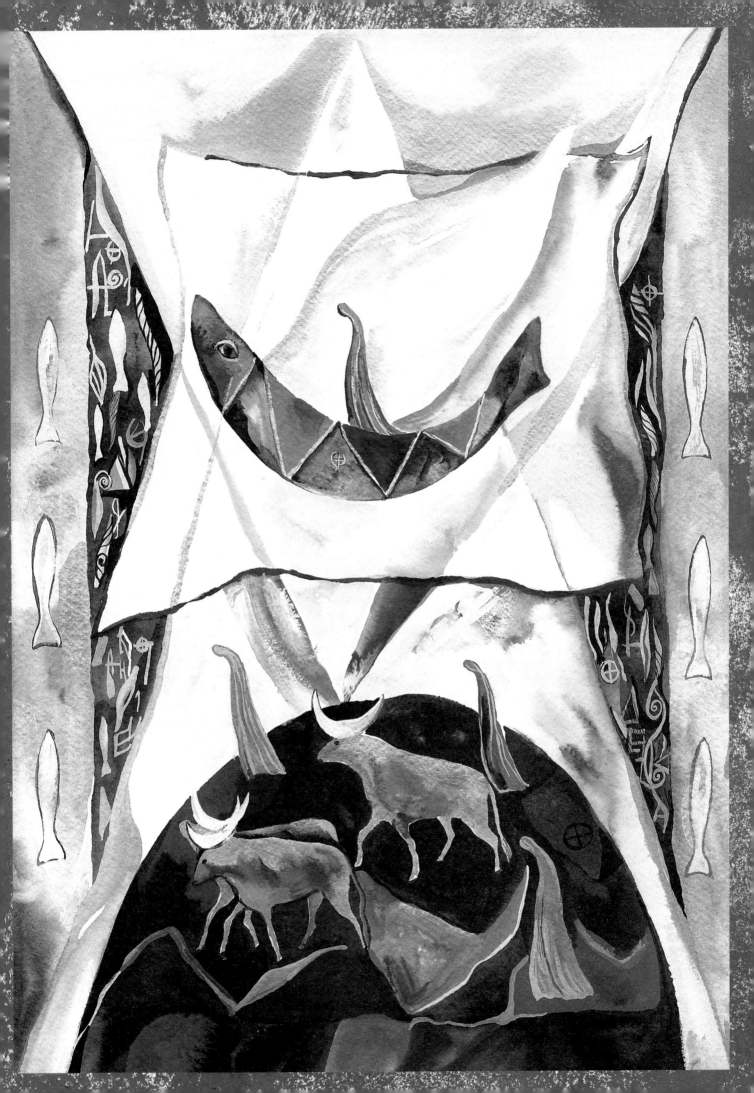